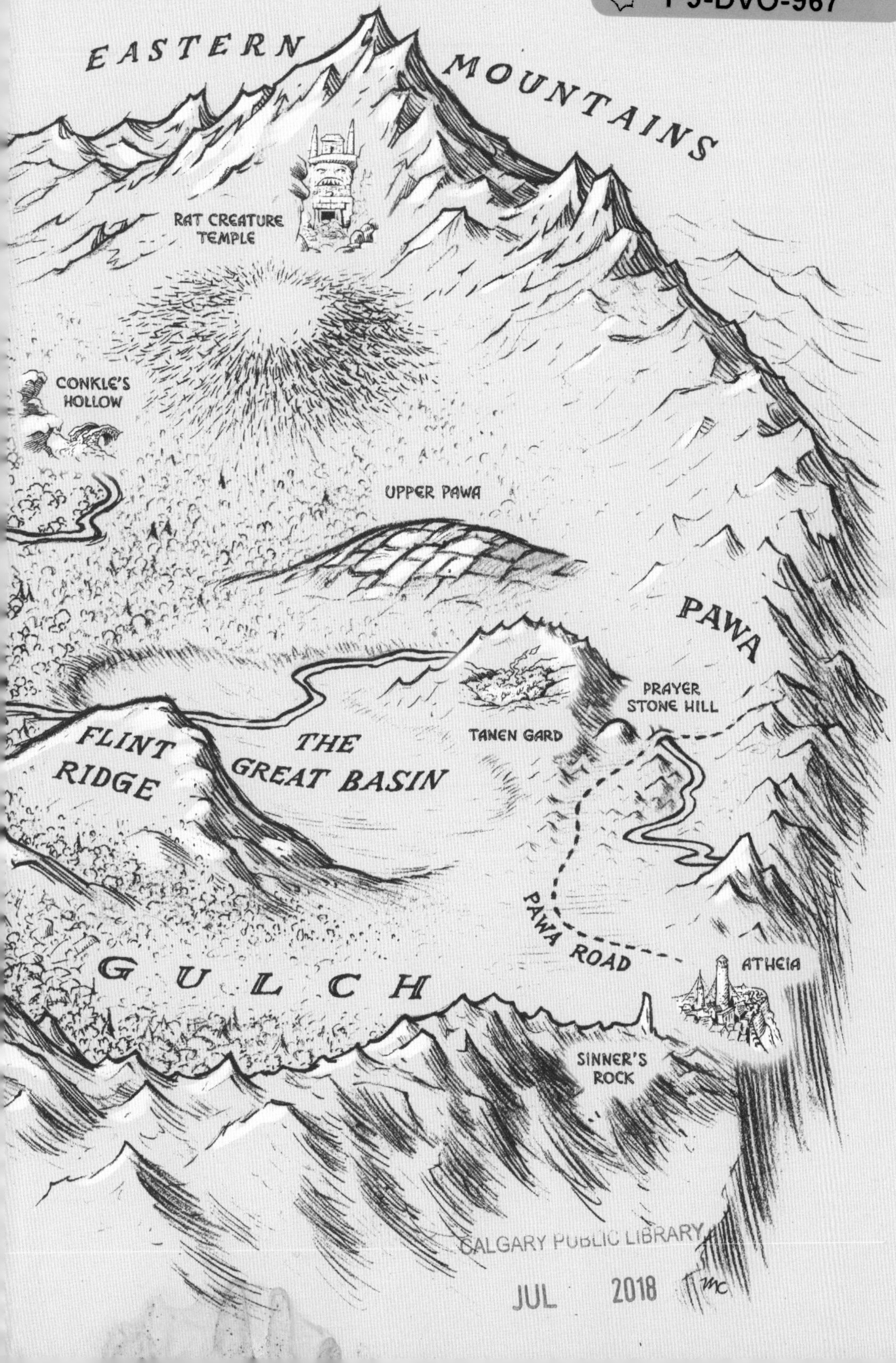

EASTERN MOUNTAINS
RAT CREATURE TEMPLE
CONKLE'S HOLLOW
UPPER PAWA
PAWA
PRAYER STONE HILL
TANEN GARD
FLINT RIDGE
THE GREAT BASIN
PAWA ROAD
ATHEIA
GULCH
SINNER'S ROCK

Dreaming of Harvestar

ACCLAIM FOR JEFF SMITH'S

Named an all time top ten graphic novel by **Time** *magazine.*

"As sweeping as the 'Lord of the Rings' cycle, but much funnier." —**Andrew Arnold, Time.com**

★*"This is first-class kid lit: exciting, funny, scary, and resonant enough that it will stick with readers for a long time."* —**Publishers Weekly**, *starred review*

"One of the best kids' comics ever." —**Vibe** *magazine*

*"***BONE** *is storytelling at its best, full of endearing, flawed characters whose adventures run the gamut from hilarious whimsy . . . to thrilling drama."* —**Entertainment Weekly**

"[This] sprawling, mythic comic is spectacular." —**SPIN** *magazine*

Rock Jaw
Master of the Eastern Border

OTHER **BONE** BOOKS

Out from Boneville

The Great Cow Race

Eyes of the Storm

The Dragonslayer

BONE

ROCK JAW
Master of the Eastern Border

BY JEFF SMITH

WITH COLOR BY STEVE HAMAKER

graphix

An Imprint of
SCHOLASTIC

Library of Congress Catalog Card Number 95068403.

ISBN-13 978-0-439-70627-8 — ISBN-10 0-439-70627-0 (hardcover)

ISBN 0-439-70636-X (paperback)

ACKNOWLEDGMENTS

Harvestar Family Crest designed by Charles Vess

Map of *The Valley* by Mark Crilley

Color by Steve Hamaker

20 19 18 17 16   18 17/0

First Scholastic edition, February 2007

Book design by David Saylor

Printed in Malaysia 108

This book is for Krishna and Avaday Iyer

CONTENTS

- CHAPTER ONE -

ROQUE JA - 1

- CHAPTER TWO -

THE ORPHANS - - - - - - - - - - - - - - - 23

- CHAPTER THREE -

RAT CREATURE TEMPLE - - - - - - - - - - - 45

- CHAPTER FOUR -

GHOST CIRCLES - - - - - - - - - - - - - - - 67

- CHAPTER FIVE -

CALL OF THE WILD - - - - - - - - - 93

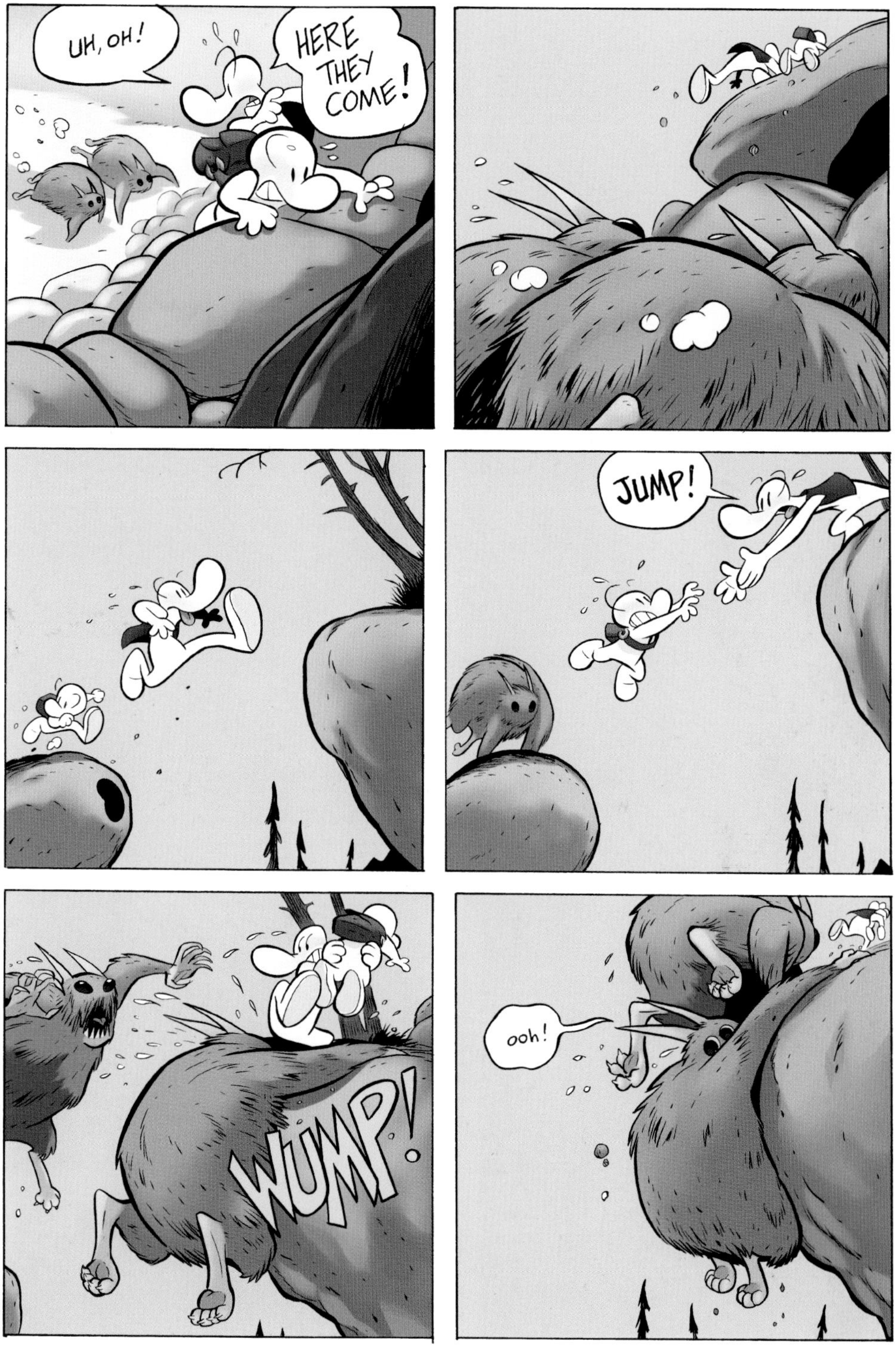
UH, OH!
HERE THEY COME!
JUMP!
WUMP!
ooh!

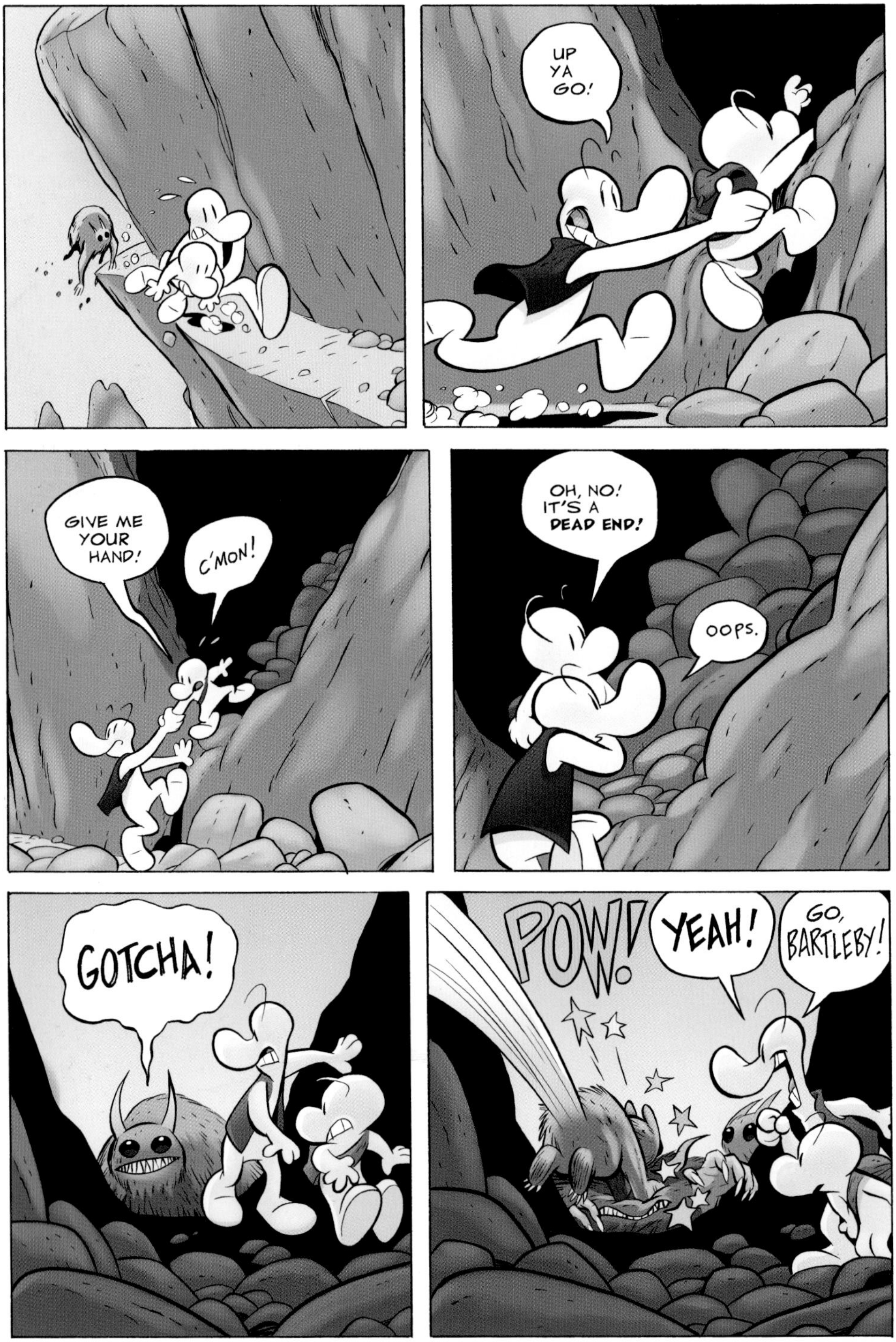
UP YA GO!
GIVE ME YOUR HAND!
C'MON!
OH, NO! IT'S A **DEAD END!**
OOPS.
GOTCHA!
POW!
YEAH!
GO, BARTLEBY!

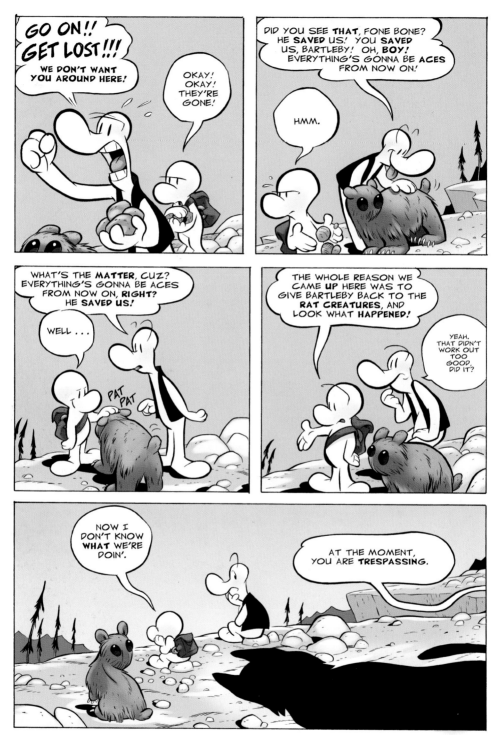

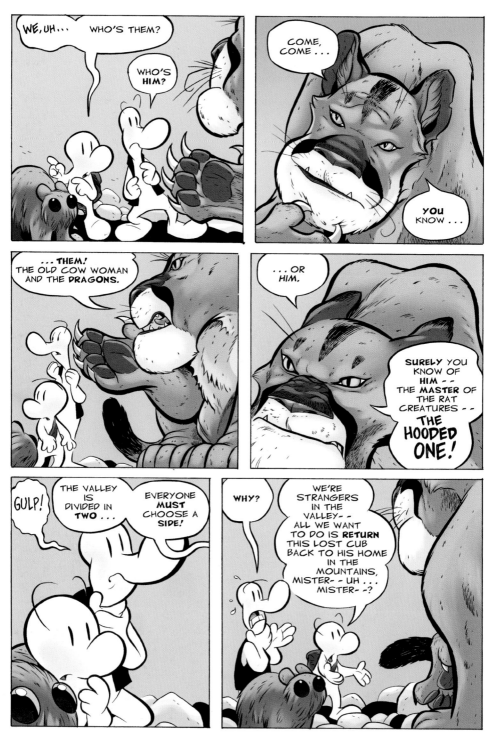

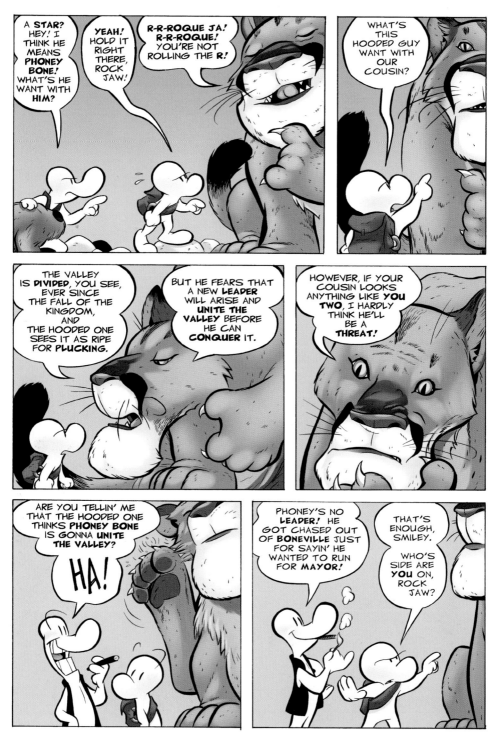

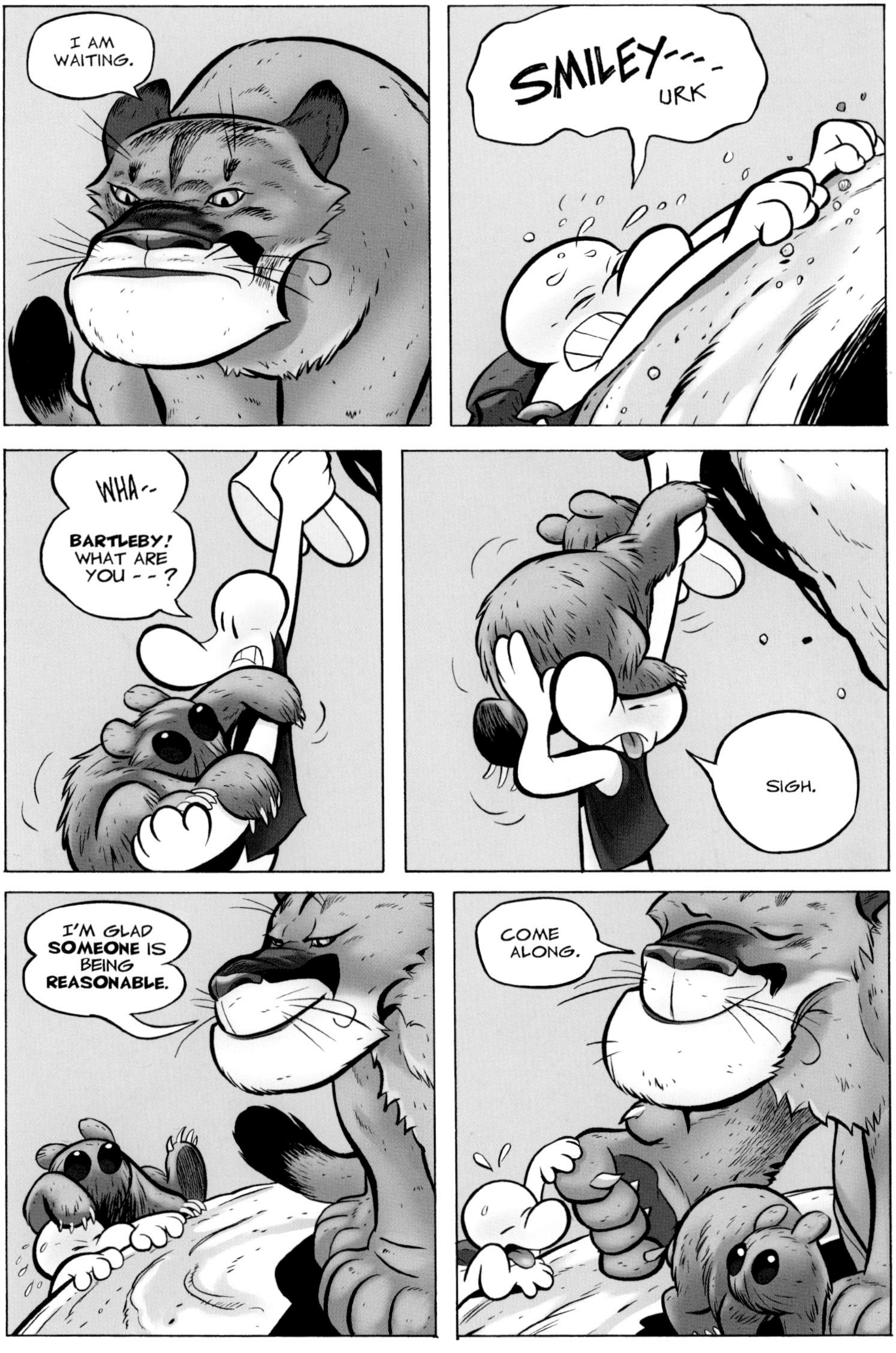
I AM WAITING.
SMILEY----
URK
WHA--
BARTLEBY! WHAT ARE YOU --?
SIGH.
I'M GLAD SOMEONE IS BEING REASONABLE.
COME ALONG.

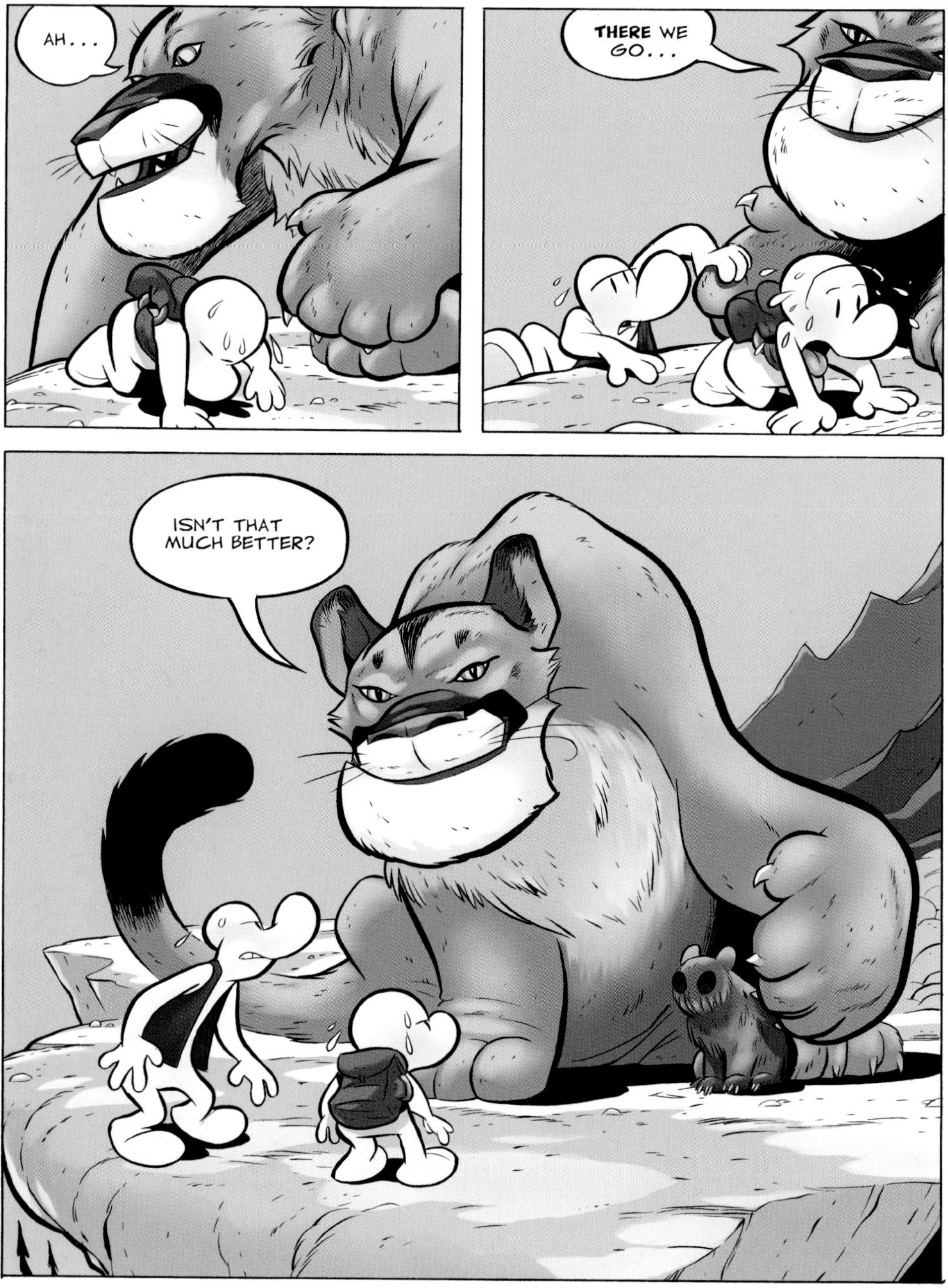
AH...
THERE WE GO...
ISN'T THAT MUCH BETTER?

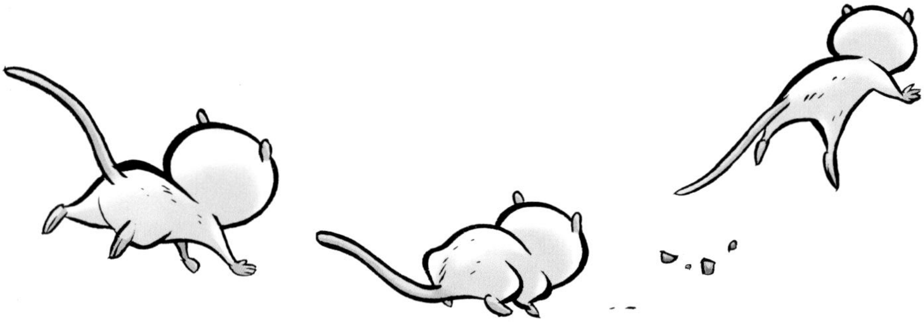

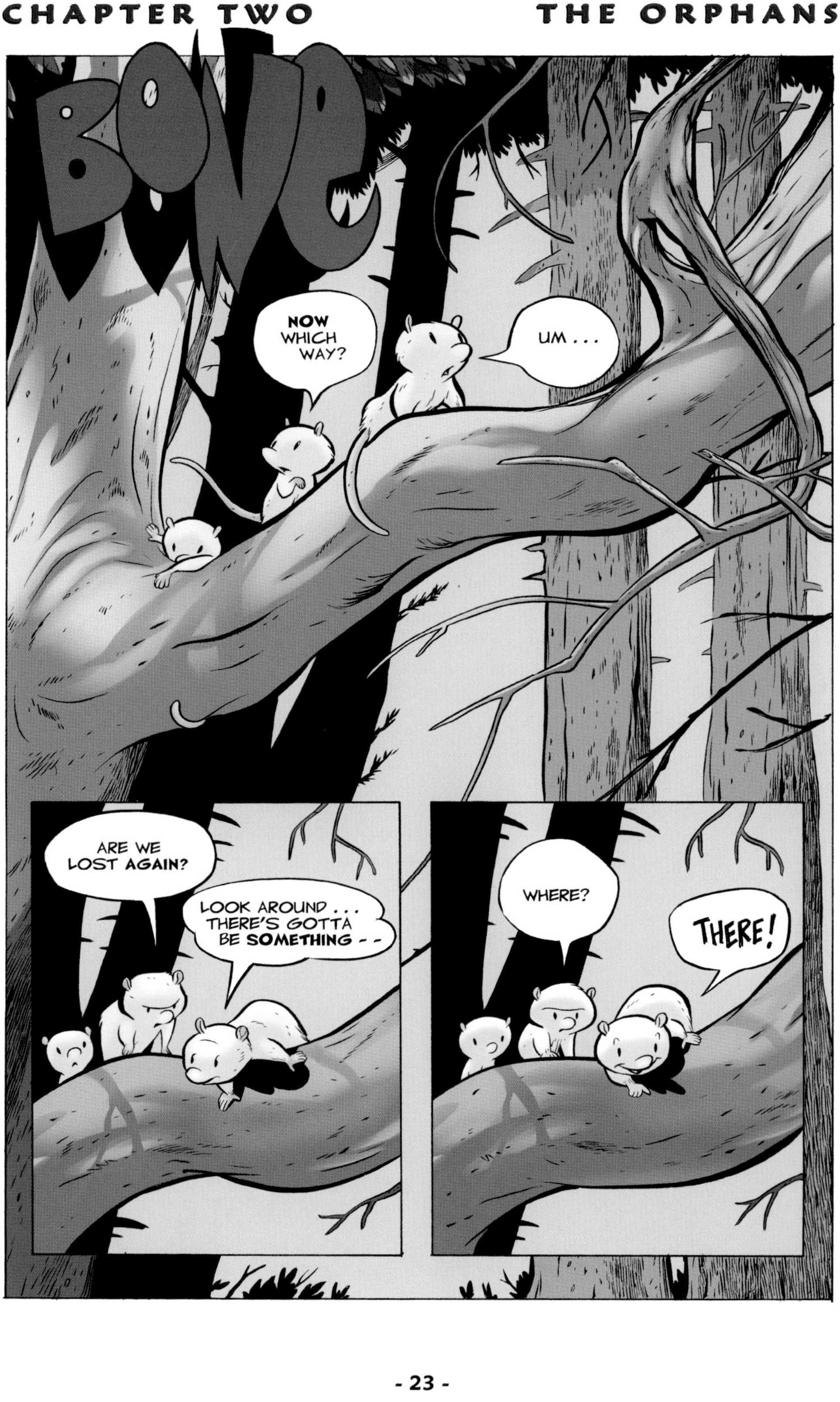
BONE
NOW WHICH WAY?
UM . . .
ARE WE LOST AGAIN?
LOOK AROUND . . . THERE'S GOTTA BE SOMETHING - -
WHERE?
THERE!

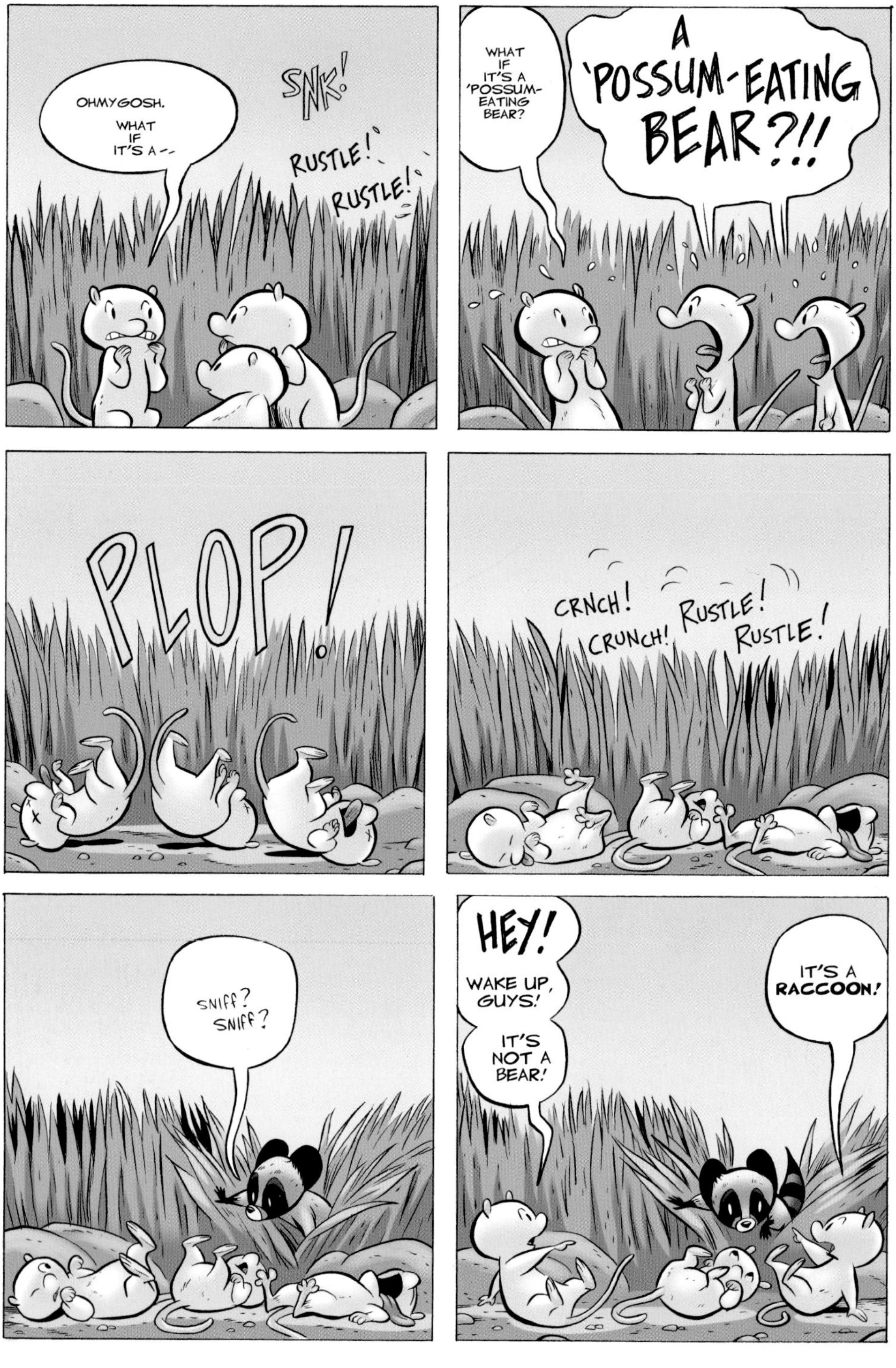
OHMYGOSH. WHAT IF IT'S A--
SNK!
RUSTLE!
RUSTLE!
WHAT IF IT'S A 'POSSUM-EATING BEAR?
A 'POSSUM-EATING BEAR?!!
PLOP!
CRNCH!
CRUNCH!
RUSTLE!
RUSTLE!
SNIFF? SNIFF?
HEY!
WAKE UP, GUYS!
IT'S NOT A BEAR!
IT'S A RACCOON!

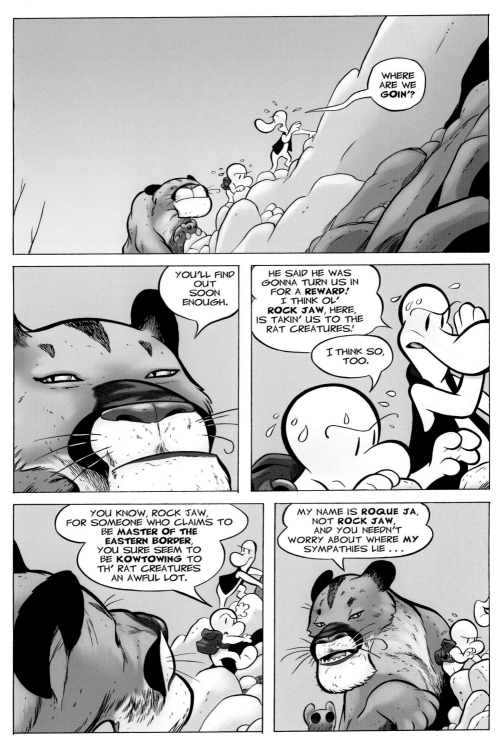

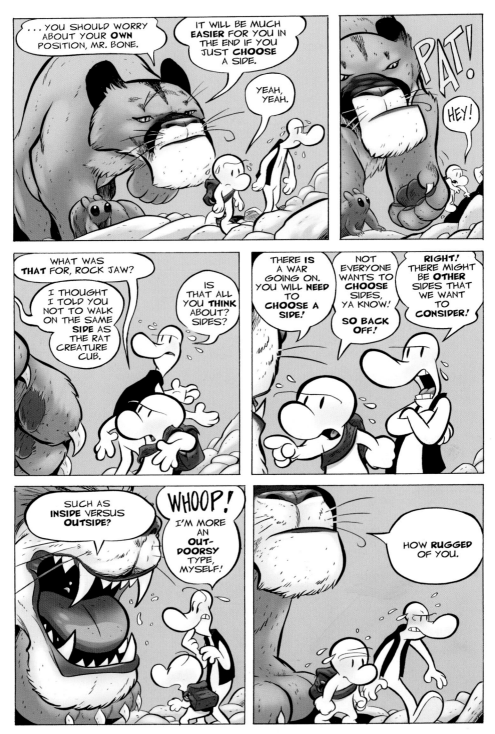

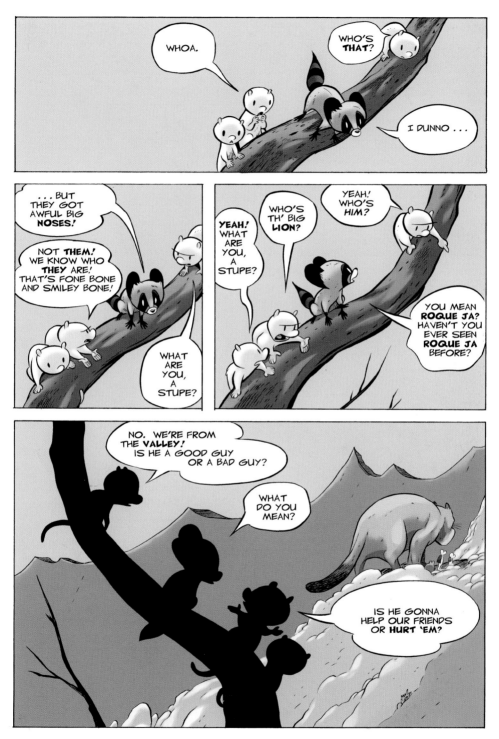

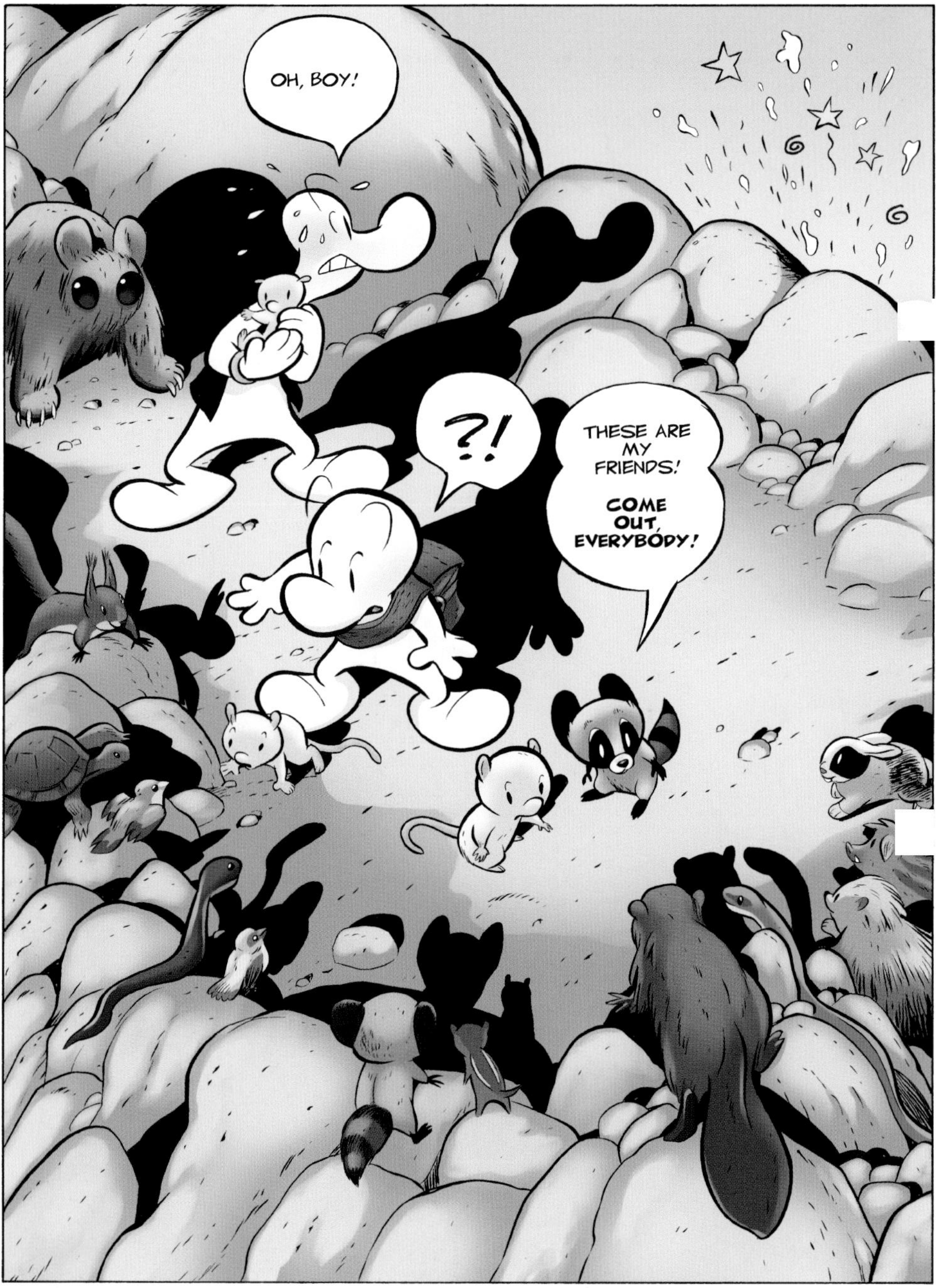
OH, BOY!
?!
THESE ARE MY FRIENDS!
COME OUT, EVERYBODY!

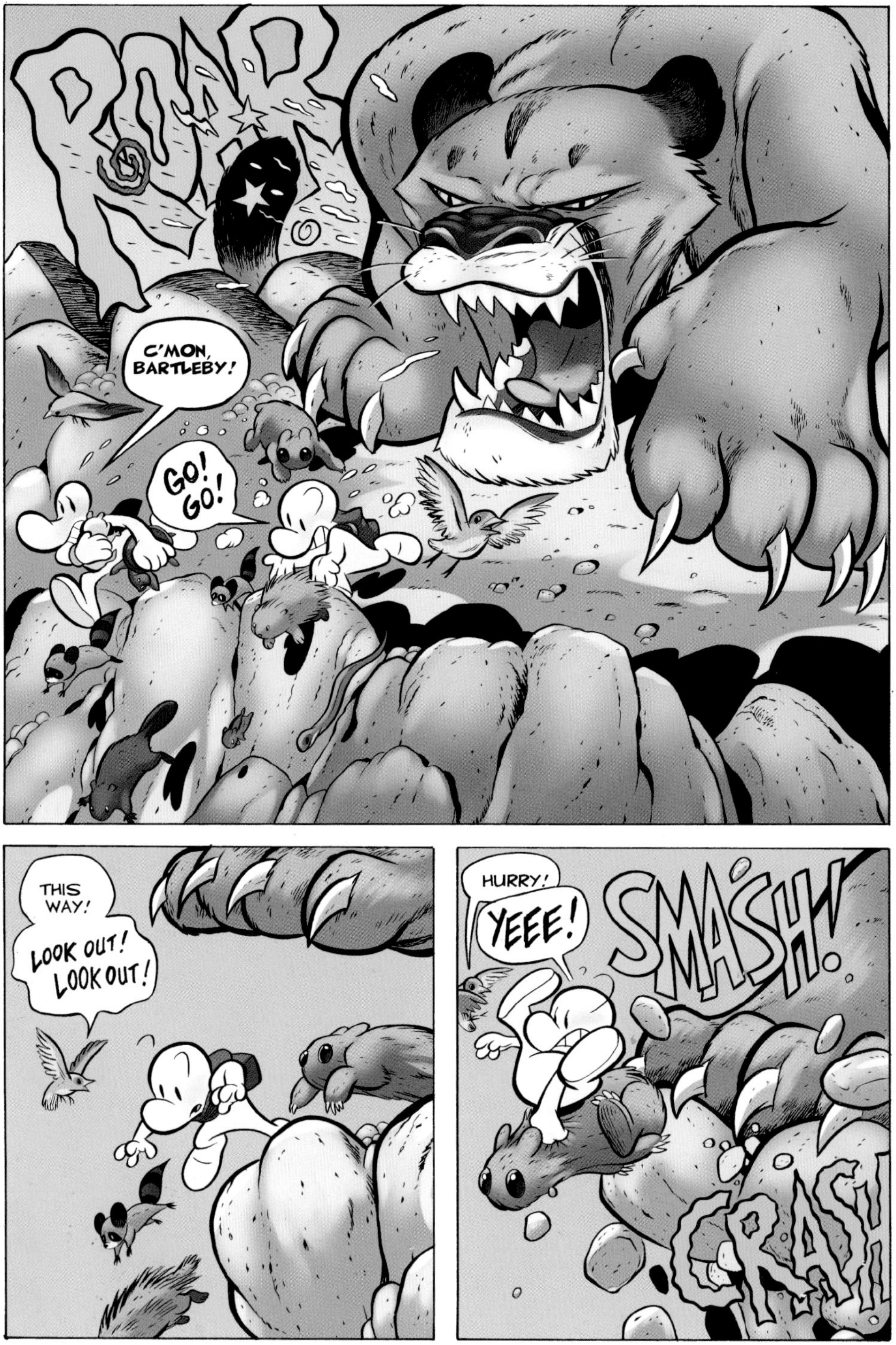
ROAR
C'MON, BARTLEBY!
GO! GO!
THIS WAY!
LOOK OUT! LOOK OUT!
HURRY!
YEEE!
SMASH!
CRASH

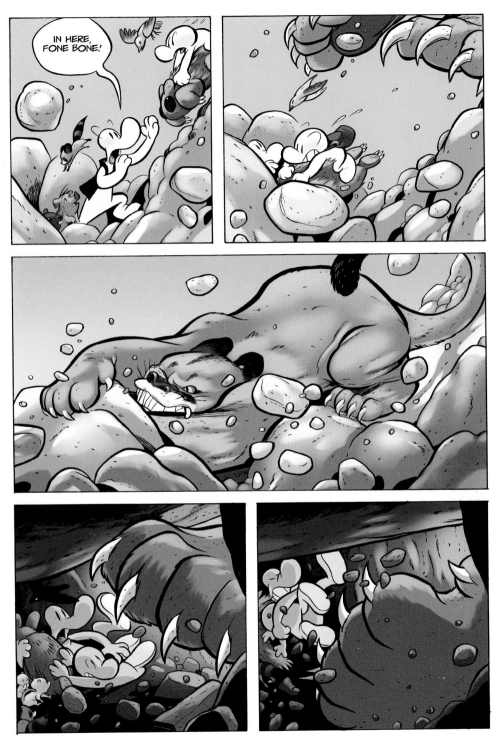

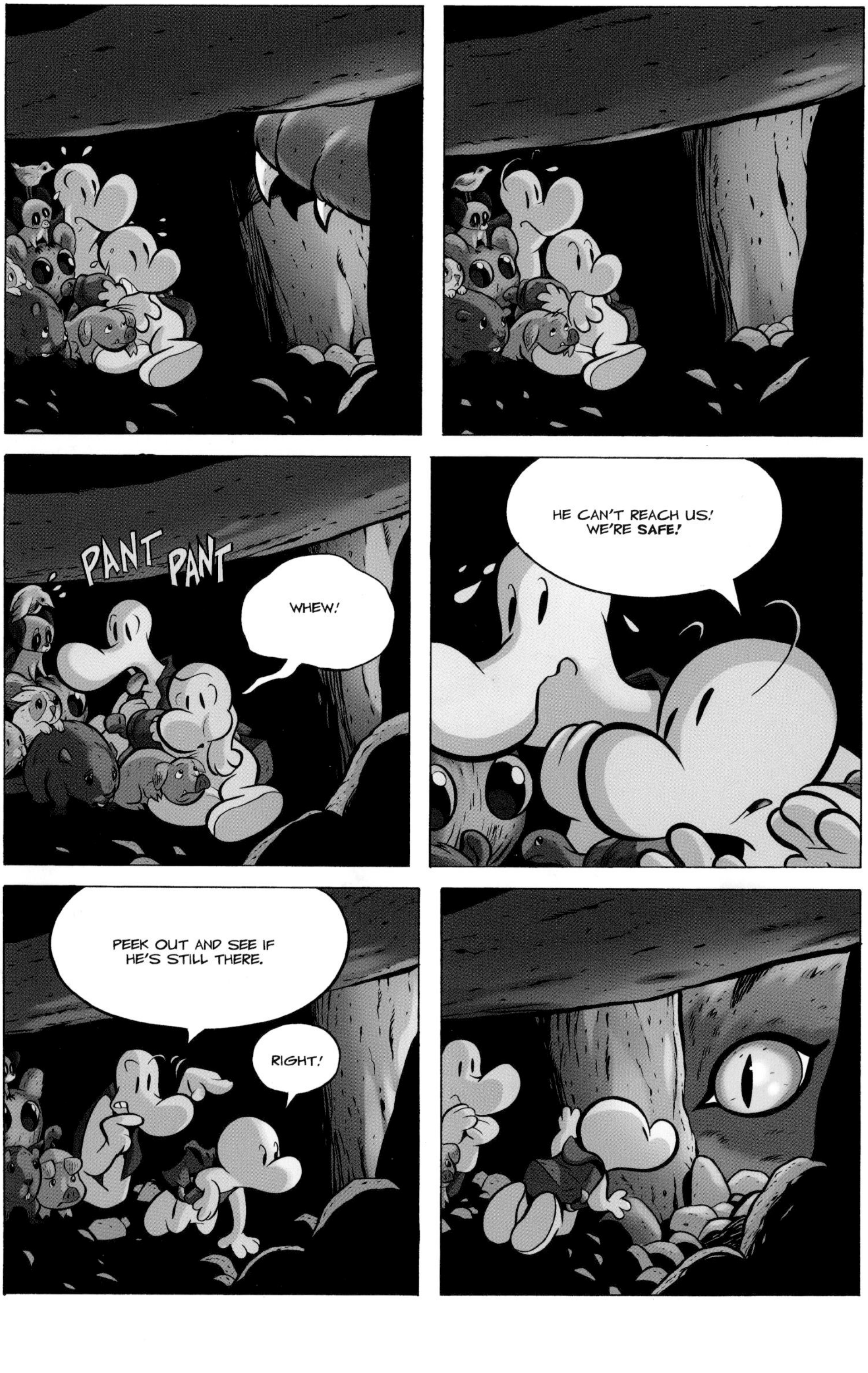
PANT PANT
WHEW!
HE CAN'T REACH US! WE'RE SAFE!
PEEK OUT AND SEE IF HE'S STILL THERE.
RIGHT!

SKRITCH!

WATCH IT. WE'RE IN SOME HUGE OPEN SPACE NOW.

SKRITCH

JUST A LITTLE FARTHER! WE'RE ALMOST THERE!

I HOPE SO. IT'S GETTIN' A LITTLE **STUFFY** IN HERE.

THIS IS IT, SMILEY! THIS IS THE **OPENING!** I'M OUTSIDE!

WHOA.

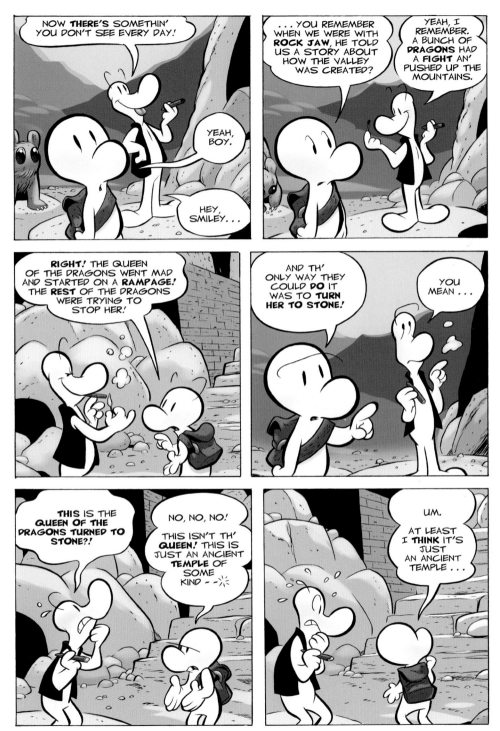

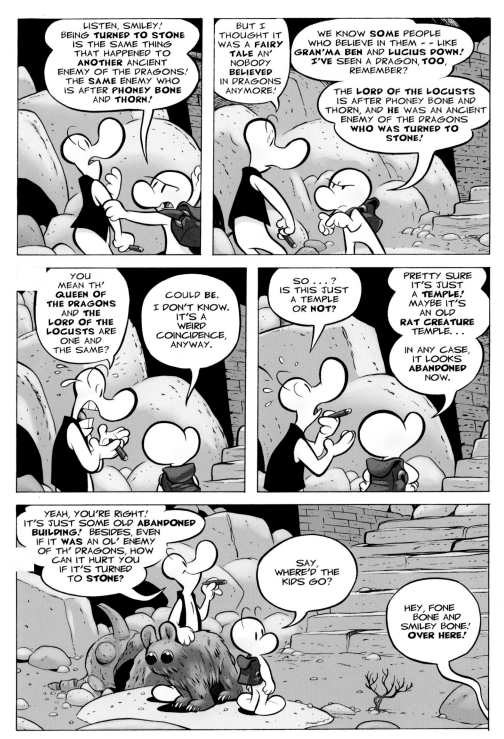

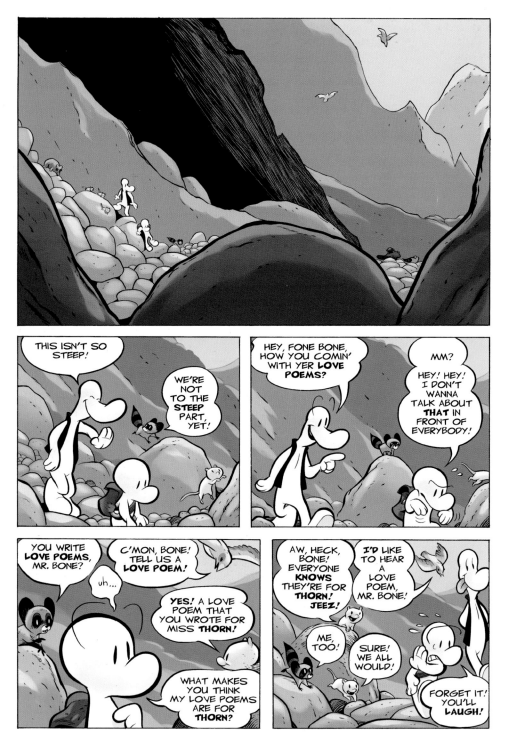

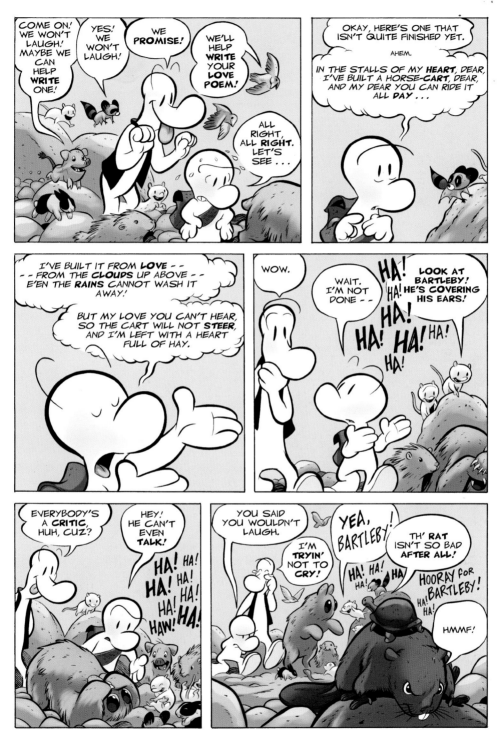

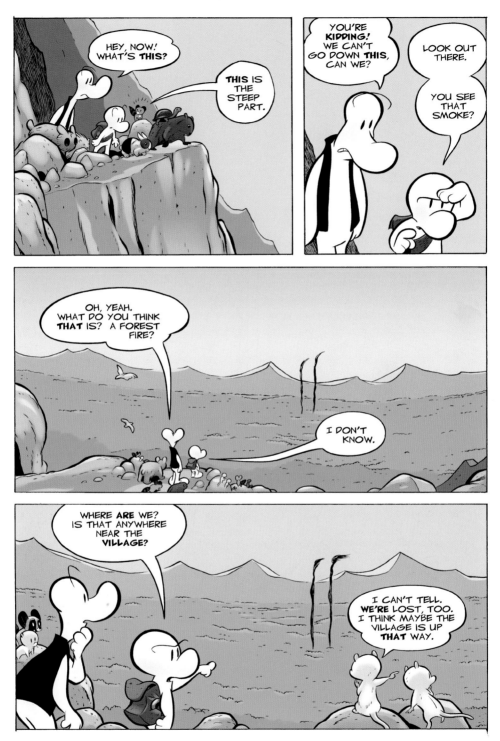

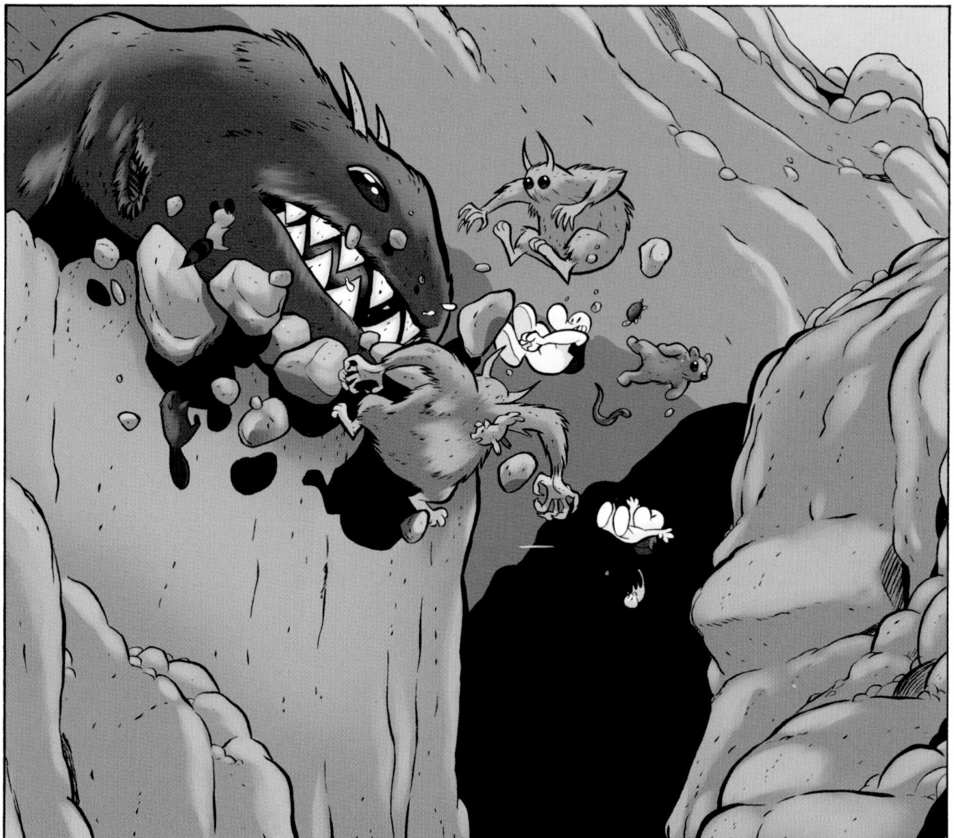
THUD!
FWAP!
SNAP!
WHERE IS EVERYBODY? IS EVERYBODY ON THE LEDGE?
CRACK
HELP!

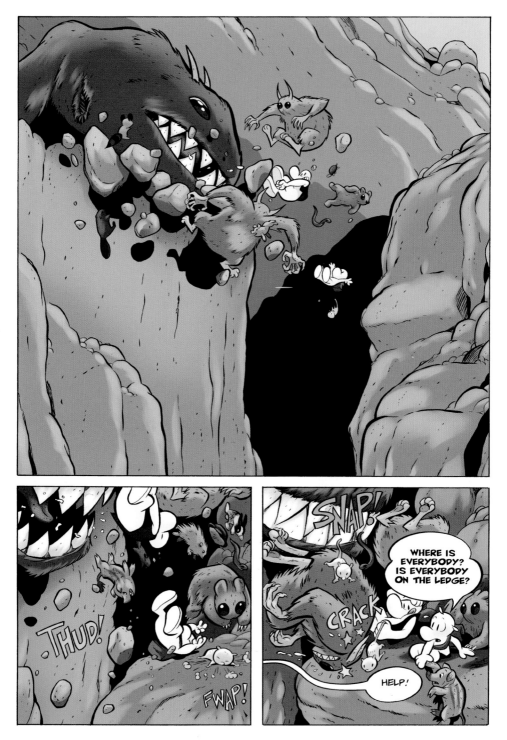

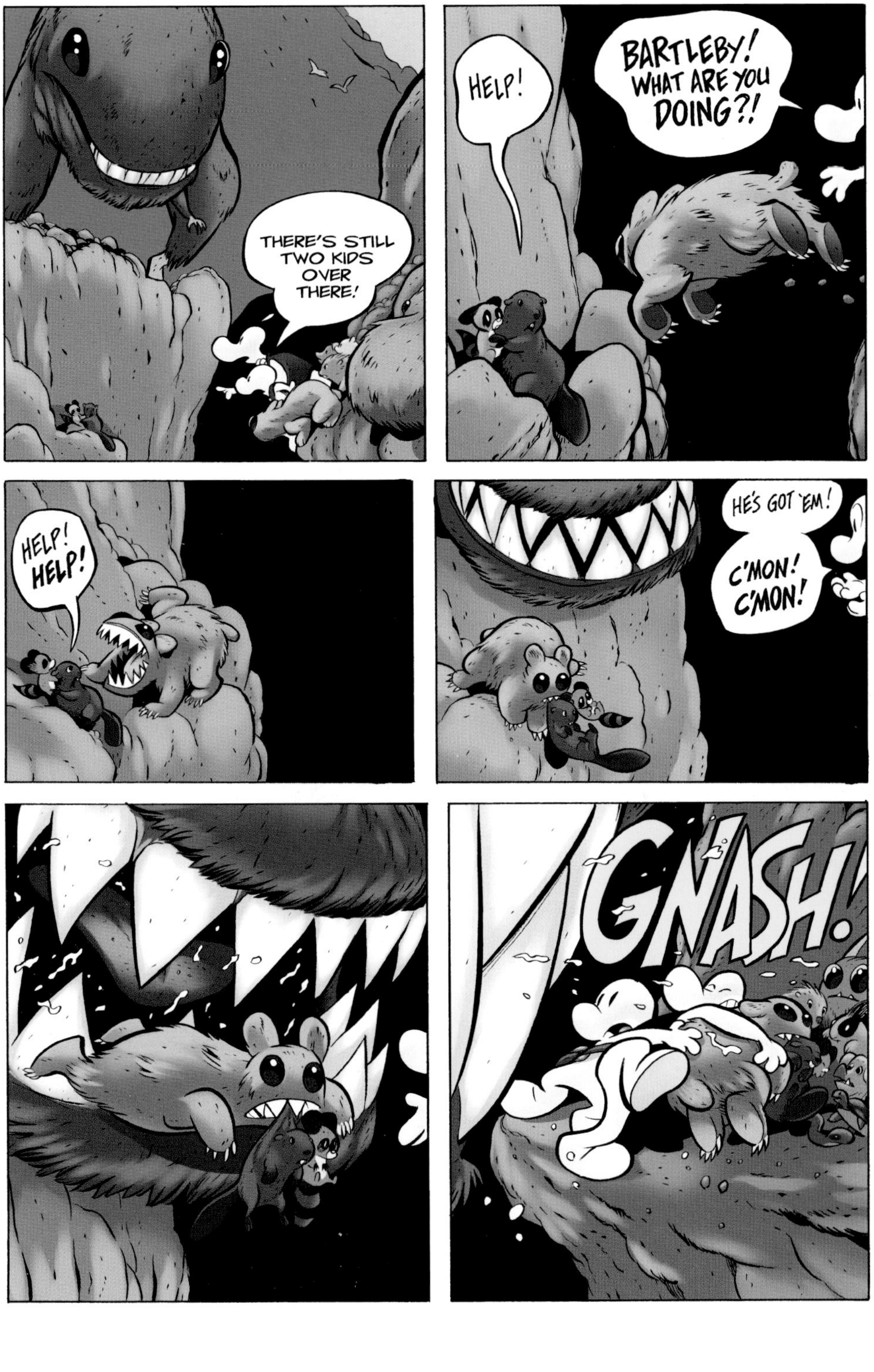
THERE'S STILL TWO KIDS OVER THERE!
HELP!
BARTLEBY! WHAT ARE YOU DOING?!
HELP! HELP!
HE'S GOT 'EM!
C'MON! C'MON!
GNASH!

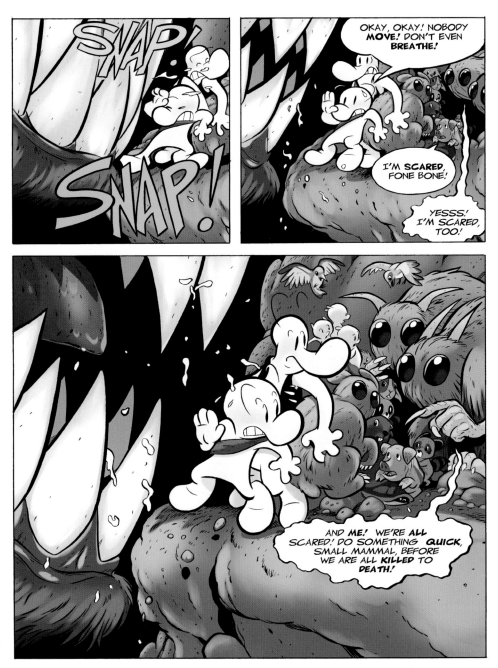

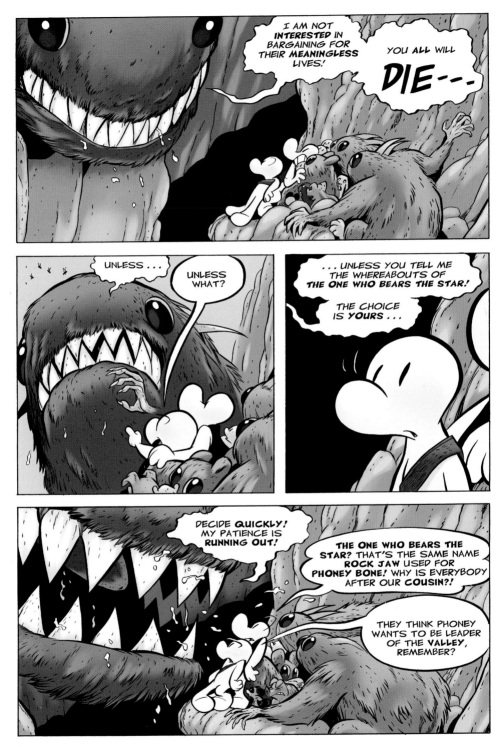

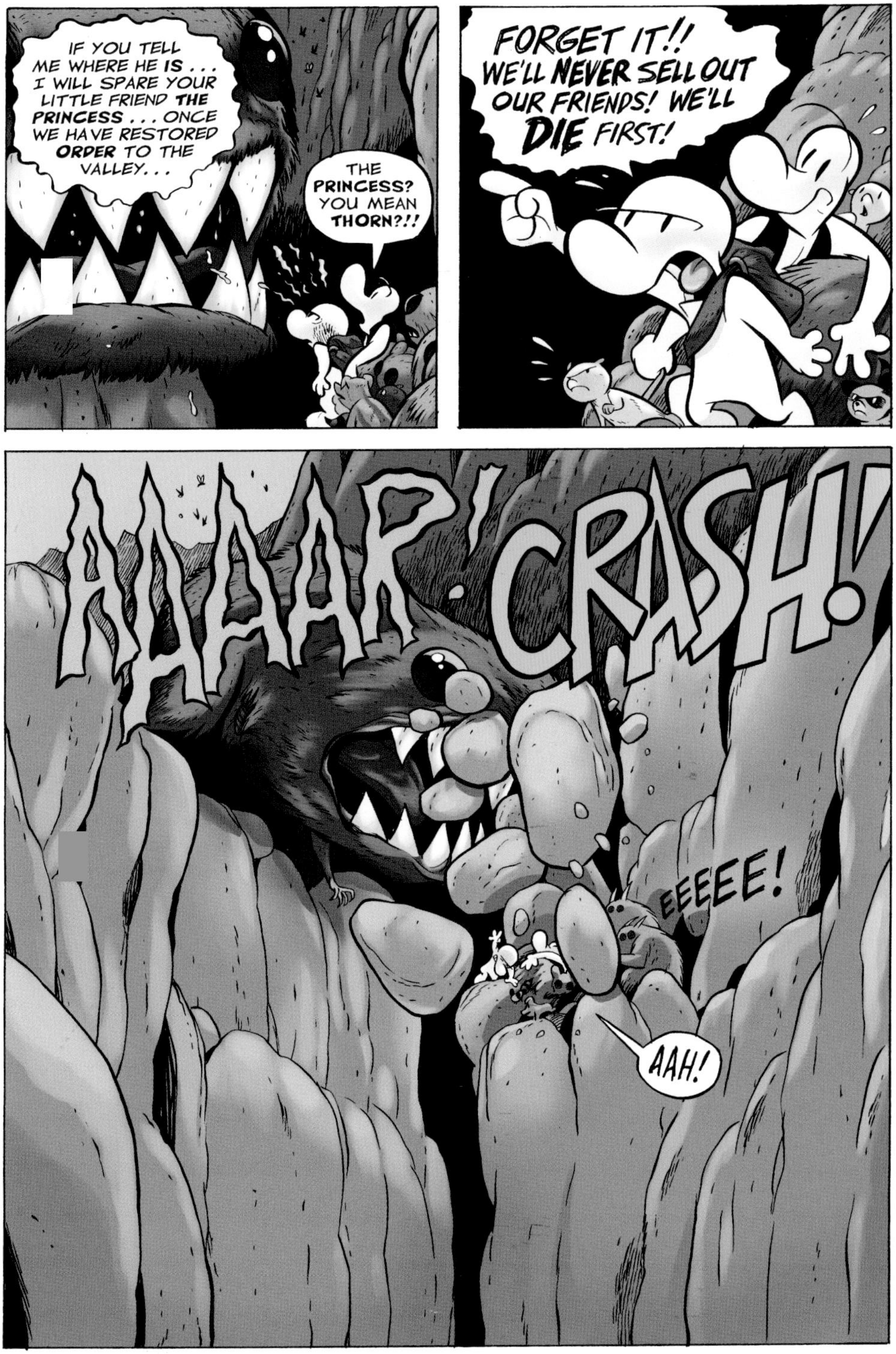
IF YOU TELL ME WHERE HE IS . . . I WILL SPARE YOUR LITTLE FRIEND THE PRINCESS . . . ONCE WE HAVE RESTORED ORDER TO THE VALLEY. . .
THE PRINCESS? YOU MEAN THORN?!!
FORGET IT!! WE'LL NEVER SELL OUT OUR FRIENDS! WE'LL DIE FIRST!
AAAAR!
CRASH!
EEEEE!
AAH!

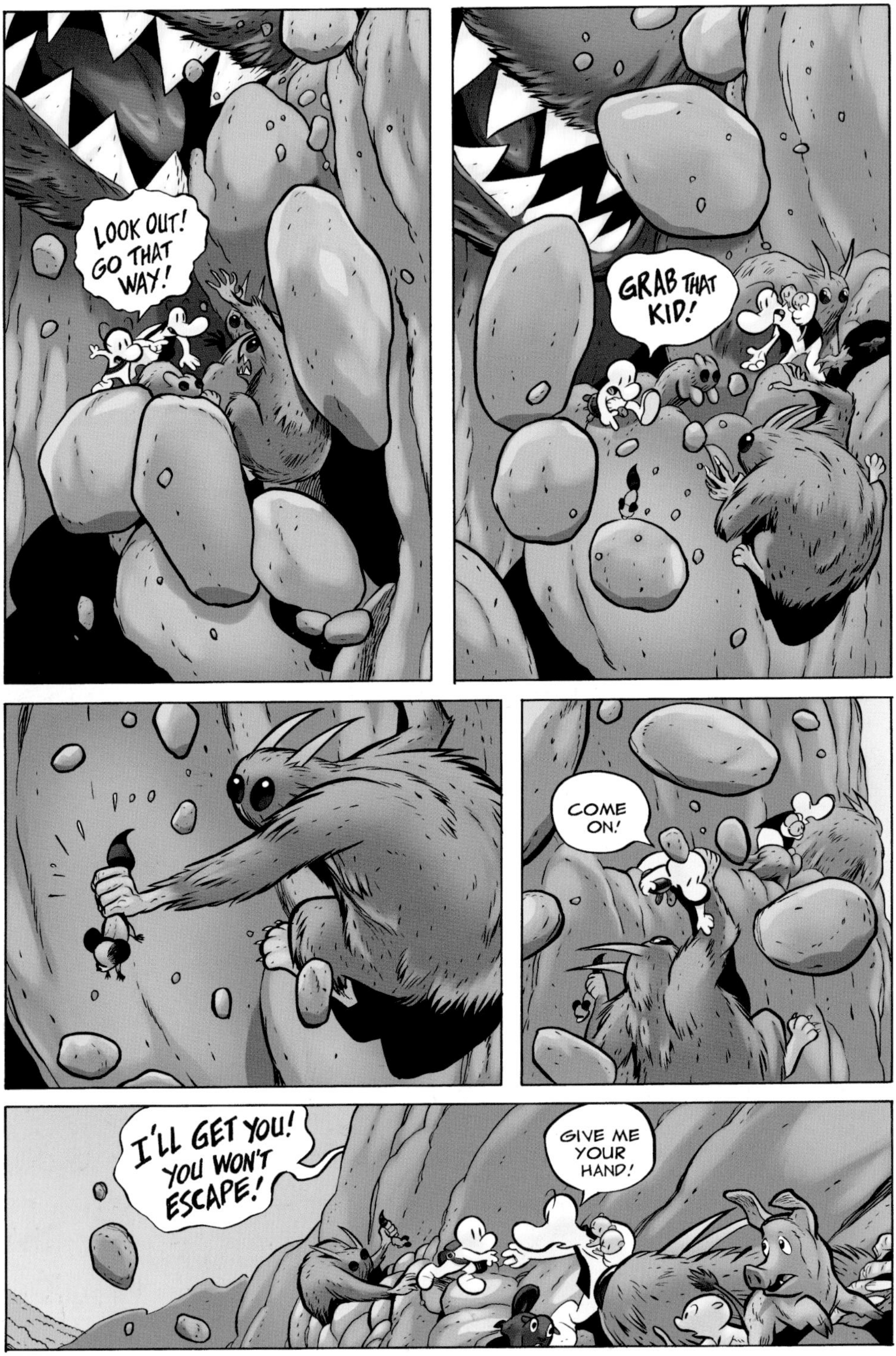
LOOK OUT! GO THAT WAY!
GRAB THAT KID!
COME ON!
I'LL GET YOU! YOU WON'T ESCAPE!
GIVE ME YOUR HAND!

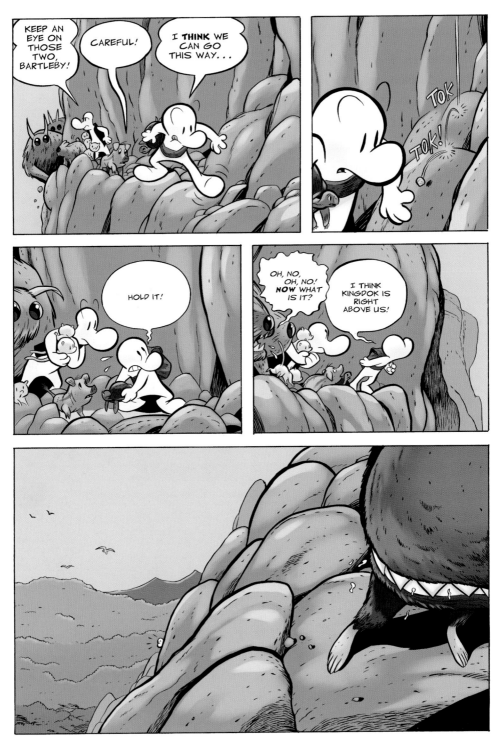

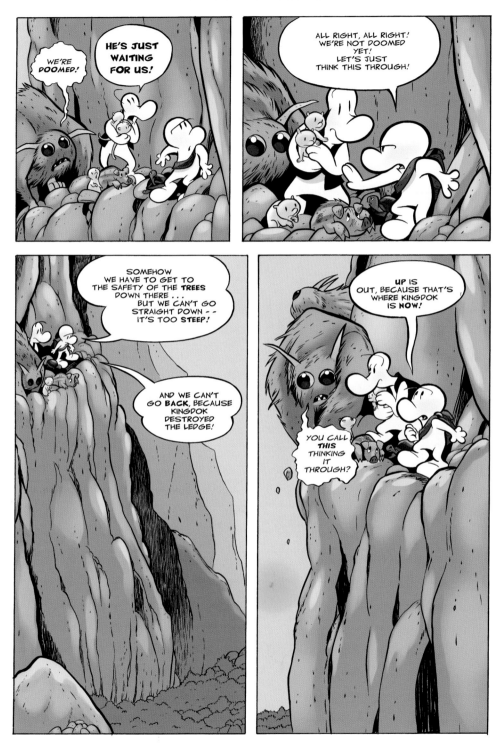

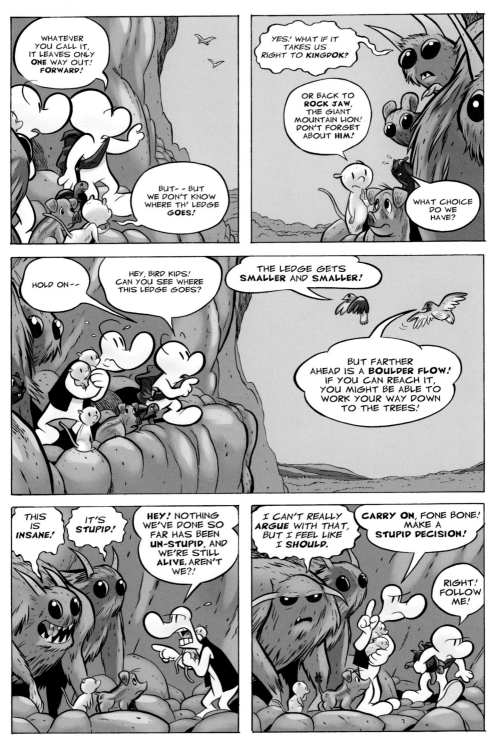

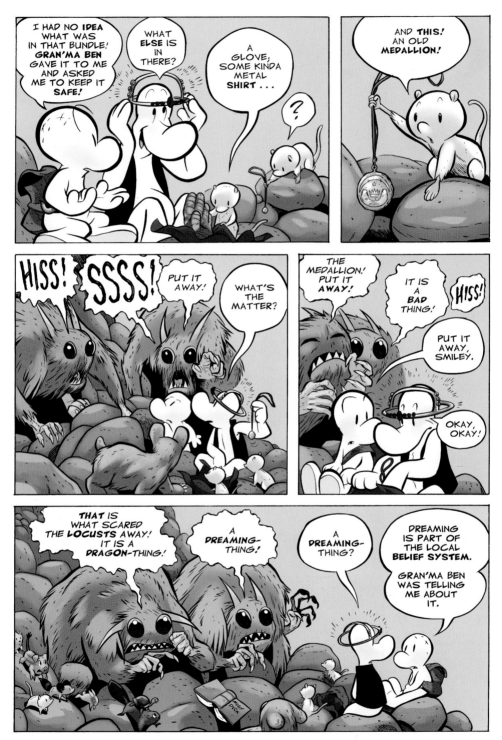

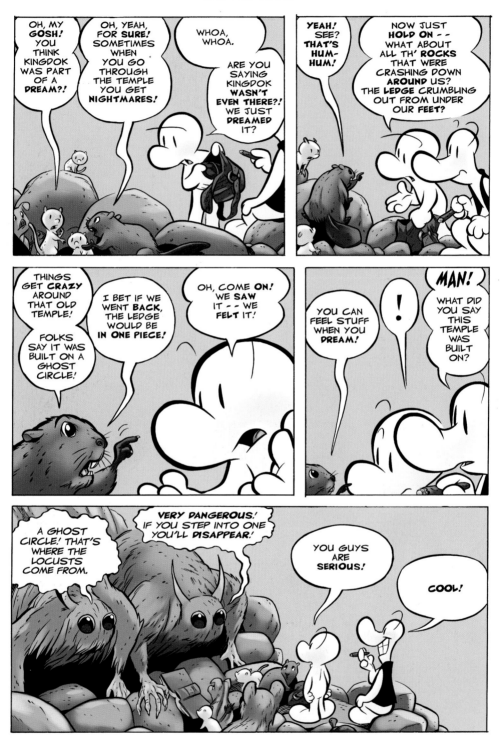

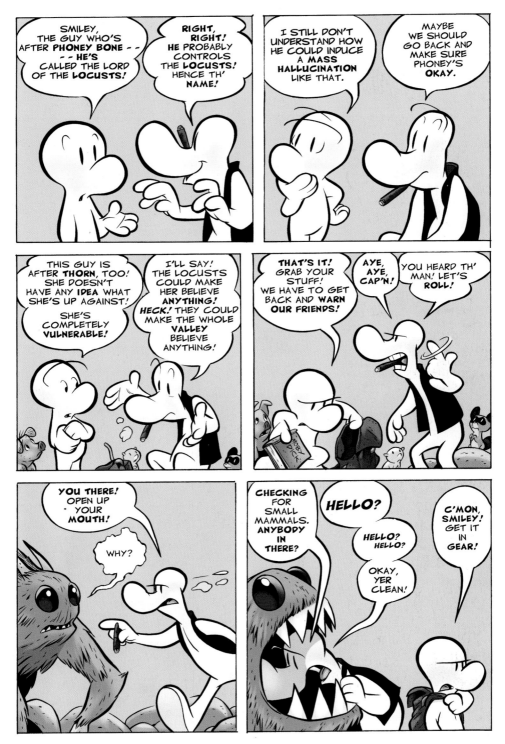

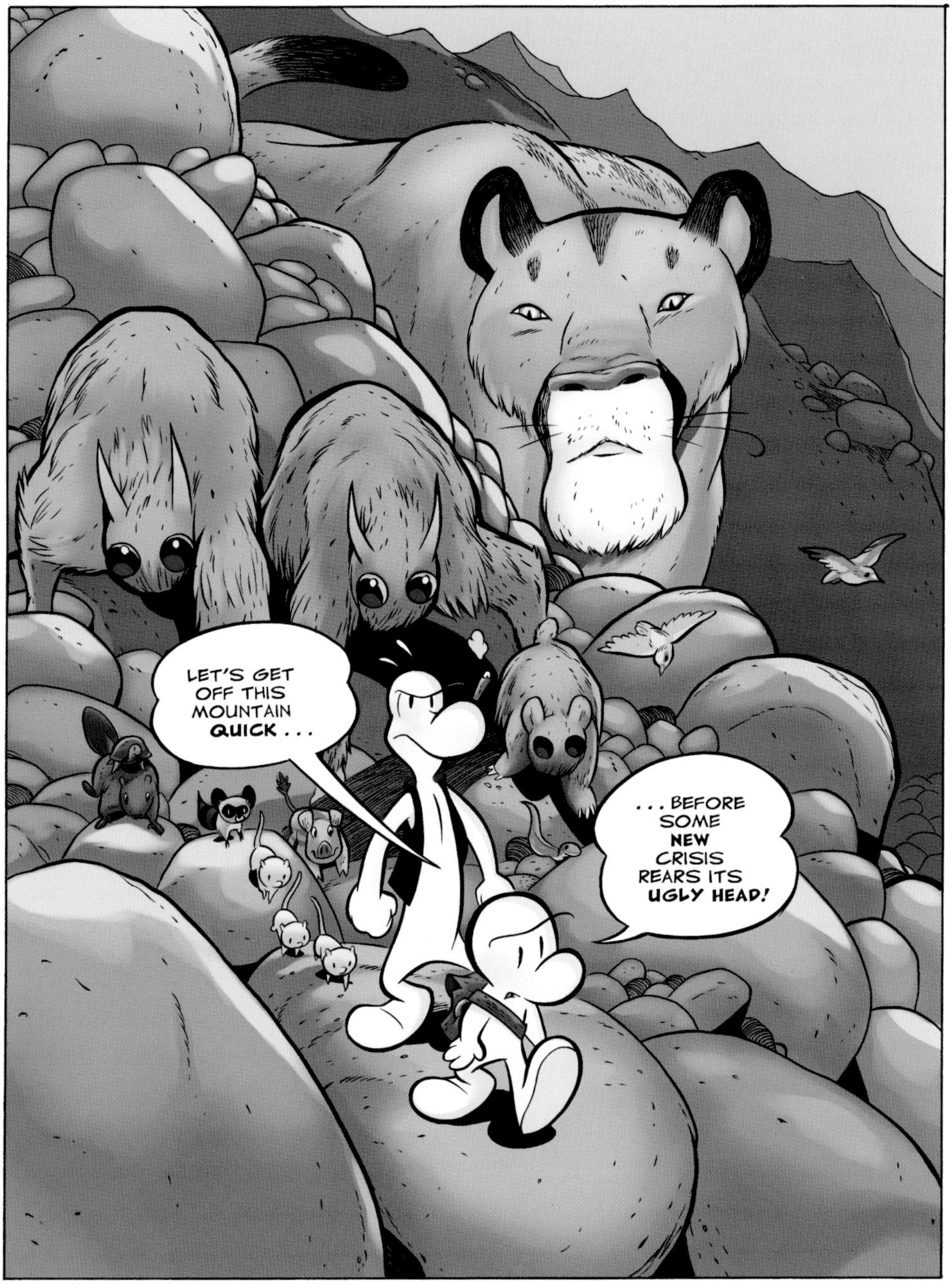
LET'S GET OFF THIS MOUNTAIN **QUICK** . . .
. . . BEFORE SOME **NEW** CRISIS REARS ITS **UGLY HEAD!**

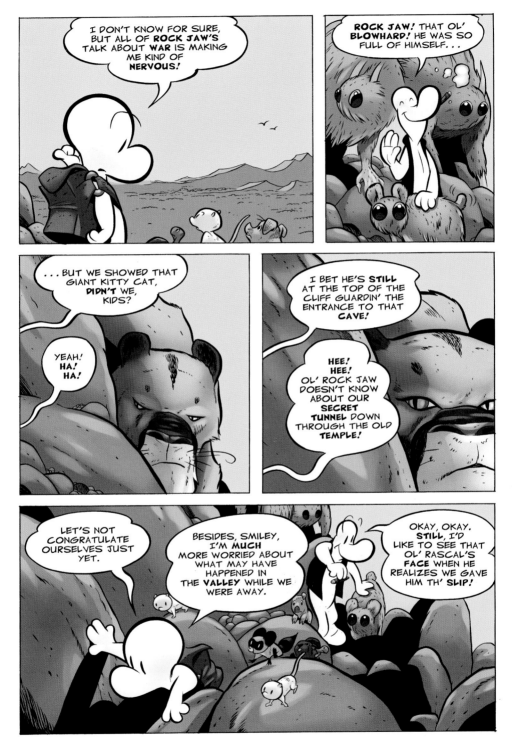

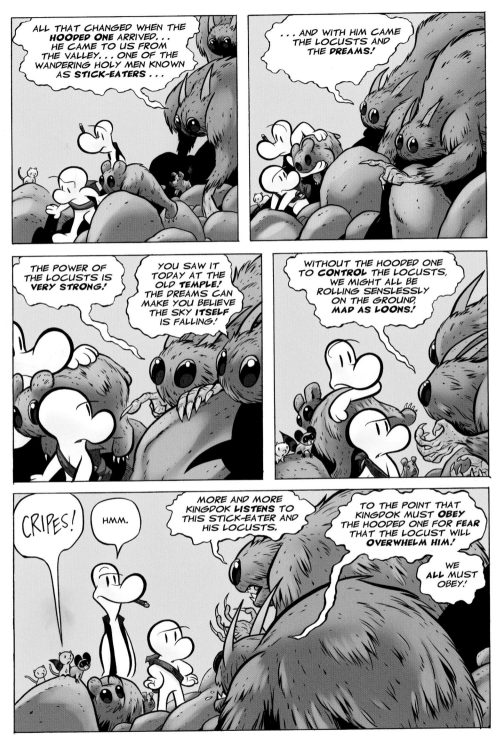

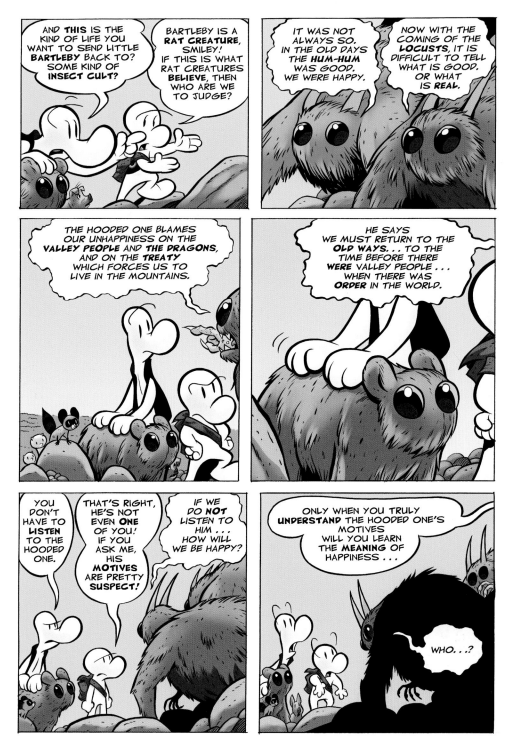

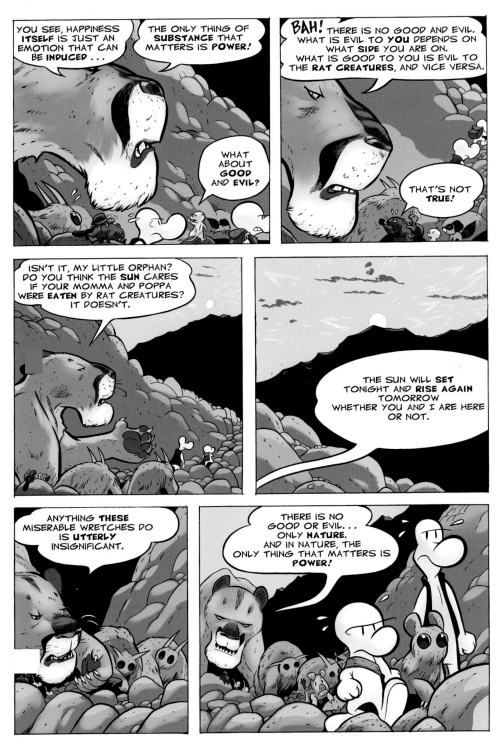

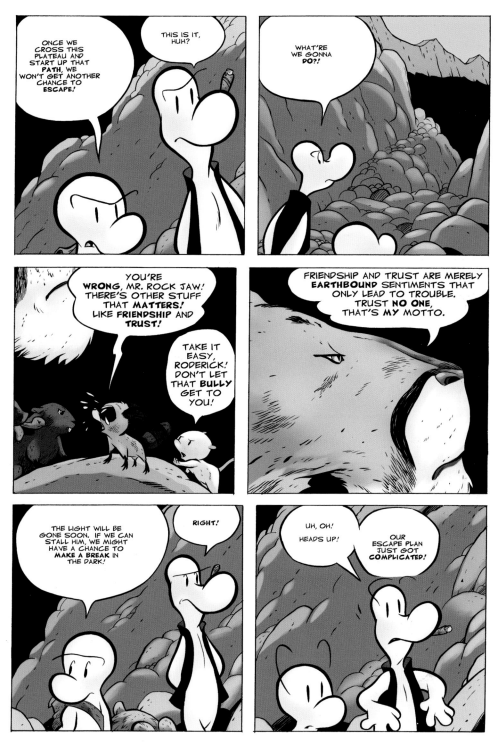

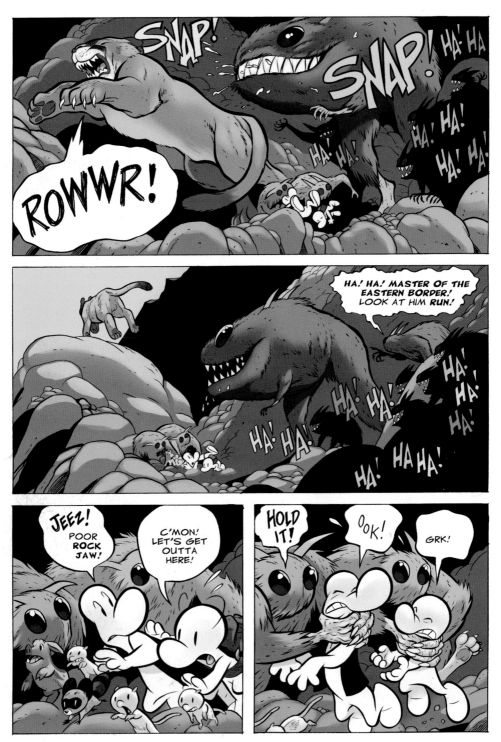

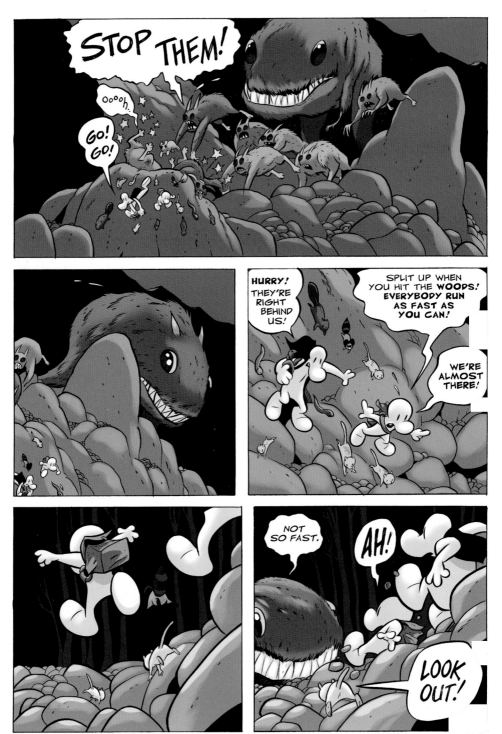

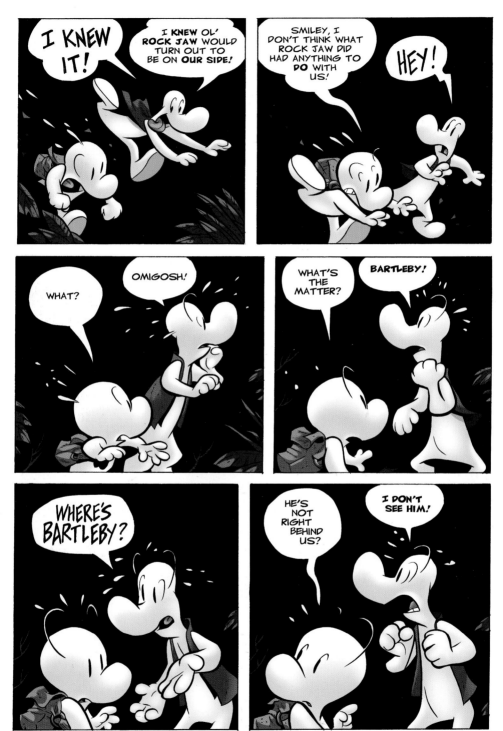

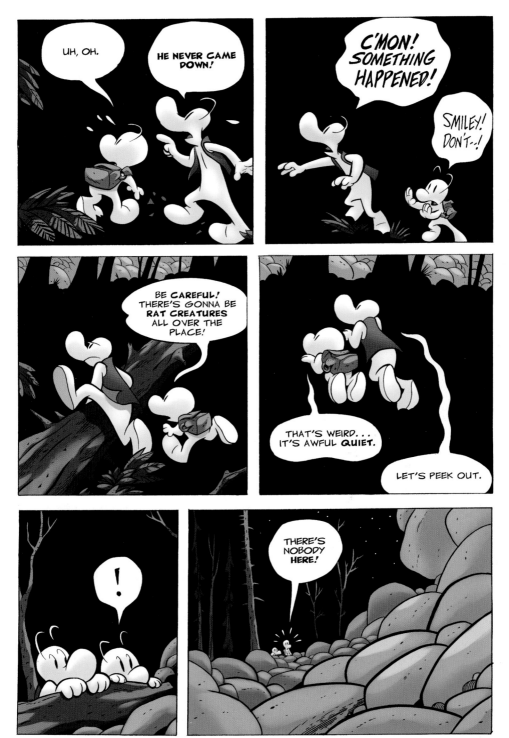

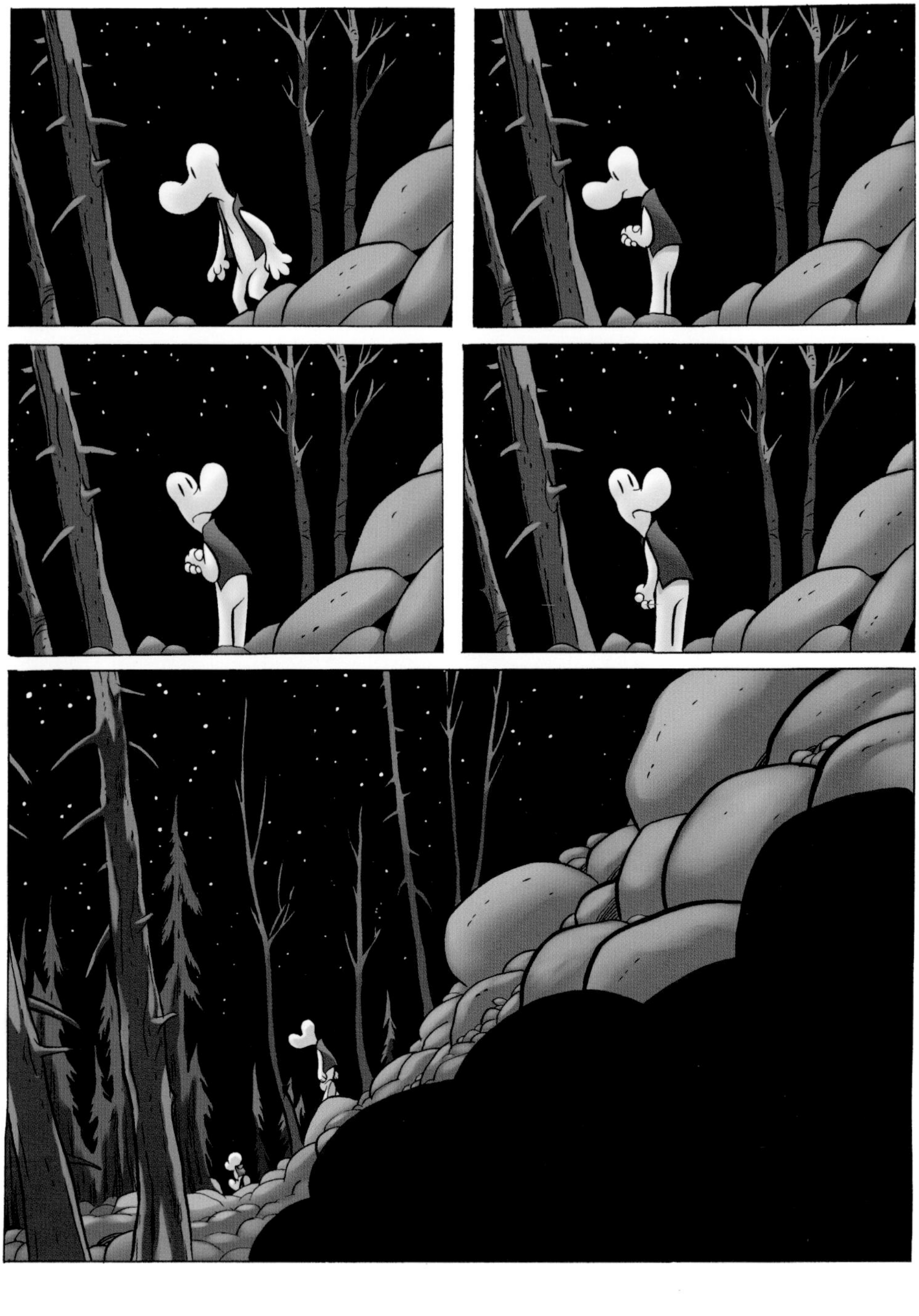

...TO BE CONTINUED.

About JEFF SMITH

JEFF SMITH was born and raised in the American Midwest and learned about cartooning from comic strips, comic books, and watching animated shorts on TV. After four years of drawing comic strips for The Ohio State University's student newspaper and co-founding Character Builders animation studio in 1986, Smith launched the comic book *BONE* in 1991. Between *BONE* and other comics projects, Smith spends much of his time on the international guest circuit promoting comics and the art of graphic novels.

More about *BONE*

An instant classic when it first appeared in the U.S. as an underground comic book in 1991, Bone has since garnered 38 international awards and sold a million copies in 15 languages. Now, Scholastic's GRAPHIX imprint is publishing full-color graphic novel editions of the nine-book *BONE* series. Look for the continuing adventures of the Bone cousins in *Old Man's Cave*.

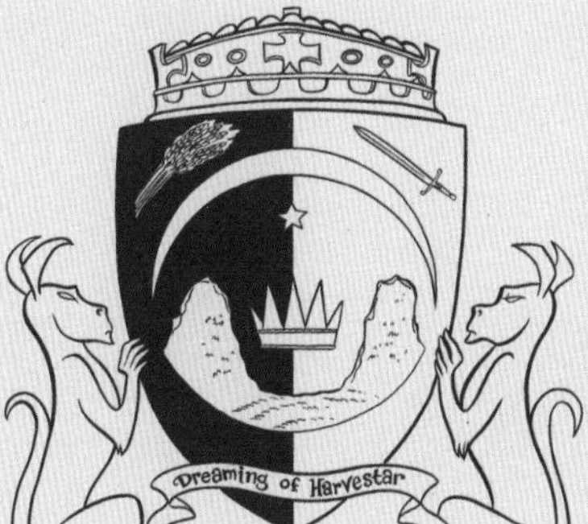
Dreaming of Harvestar

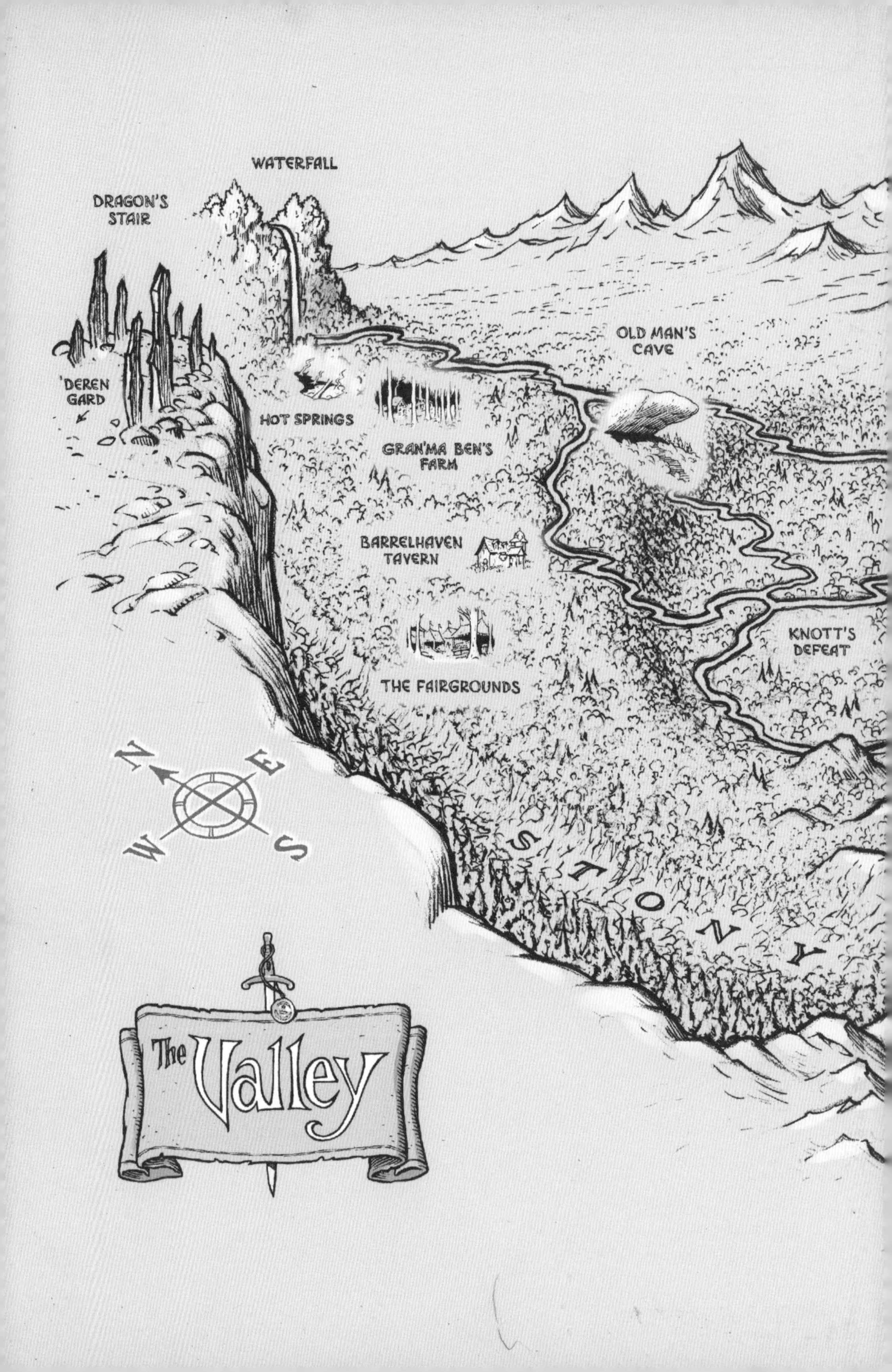

WATERFALL
DRAGON'S STAIR
DEREN GARD
HOT SPRINGS
GRAN'MA BEN'S FARM
OLD MAN'S CAVE
BARRELHAVEN TAVERN
THE FAIRGROUNDS
KNOTT'S DEFEAT
N
E
W
S
STONY
The Valley